Spaceports & Spidersilk

October 2024

Edited by
Marcie Lynn Tentchoff

Spaceports & Spidersilk
October 2024
Edited by Marcie Lynn Tentchoff

All rights reserved. No part of this publication may be reproduced or transmitted in any form or by any means, electronic or mechanical, including photocopying or recording or by any information storage and retrieval systems, without expressed written consent of the author and/or artists.

All characters herein are fictitious, and any resemblance between them and actual people is strictly coincidental.

Story and art copyrights owned by the respective authors and artists
Cover art "Nerves of Steel" by Michelle St. James
Cover design by Laura Givens

First Printing, October 2024

Hiraeth Publishing
P.O. Box 1248
Tularosa, NM 88352
www.hiraethsffh.com
e-mail: hiraethsubs@yahoo.com

Visit www.hiraethsffh.com for science fiction, fantasy, horror, scifaiku, and more. While you are there, visit the Shop for books and more! **Support the small, independent press…**

Stories

12	A Halloween Murder by David Aronlee
23	The Other World by Cheryl J. Brown
36	A Graveyard Promise by Drew Alexander Ross
49	Near and Far by Laurel Hanson
64	Trail of the Dancing Dinosaur by Pamela Lee
72	Stay Cool Danny by Hala Dika

Poetry

21	The Hungry Vampire in Space by Gary Davis
33	Pointy Things by Adele Gardner
47	Little Ghost by Margaret Zotkiewicz
61	Haiku by Lisa Timpf
	Outside the Alien's Petting Zoo by Lauren McBride
71	Wicked Woods by Leigh Therriault

Illustrations
Illustrations by Michelle St. James

90   Who's Who

SALE AT HIRAETH PUBLISHING!!!

BUY ALL THE BOOKS YOU WANT AND USE THIS 20% DISCOUNT CODE: BOOKS2024

GO TO OUR SHOP AT WWW.HIRAETHSFFH.COM

NO MASKS, NO WAITING, AND WE NEVER CLOSE!

What?

You don't have a subscription to Spaceports & Spidersilk???

(*Gasp*)

We can fix that!
Just go here and order:

https://www.hiraethsffh.com/product-page/spaceports-and-spidersilk

From the Editor

Welcome, readers, to the October 2024 issue of Spaceports & Spidersilk. As is not uncommon, I have a question for you:

What is a ghost town?

I'm sure many of you have heard the term. The definition of a ghost town seems to be a town which has, for one reason or another, lost most of its inhabitants, with only the buildings and empty streets left to testify that people used to live there at all. It was a term used a lot in movies and books about the Old West, where once busy towns were abandoned, often because the main source of jobs disappeared, as when there was no more gold left in a local mine, or the water needed to grow crops and cattle dried up.

Of course, other stories tell of ghost towns where the people left not because of a loss of revenue, but because of a physical danger, such as an increased chance of flooding, or avalanche, or worse, something or someone showing up who intended harm to the townsfolk.

But why the term "ghost town?" Is it used because the town now seems more dead than alive, or because the town is haunted by the memories of what it used to be, such that visitors can look at an old, rickety school house and barely picture the children who once played outside during recess, or glance at an old saloon, its door now hanging dusty and off kilter, and imagine they hear faded strains of piano music and dancing feet?

Or are such towns haunted by something darker than memories?

This is, let's not forget, the *October* issue. Let's go out on a bit of a limb and consider that the towns in the magazine you are holding, the one with a cover that seems to show a somewhat futuristic version of an Old Western ghost town, might be haunted by real ghosts, or perhaps by other things just as unusual.

Expect to read of dancing ghosts, spooky forests, and haunted cities and graveyards, as well as vampires, witches (or at least their familiars), aliens of various types, and creatures that defy explanation.

After all, while a ghost town may be abandoned (or nearly so) by humans, it could be a wild vacation spot for other beings.

Happy reading!

Pyra and the Tektites
Aquarium in Space

Pyra, age thirteen, is running away from home in the Asteroid Belt because she's not doing well in school. Her parents want to send her to Mars for school, and she doesn't want to go. She sneaks aboard a cargo shuttle, and falls asleep in the hold. When she awakens, she finds herself in free-fall; the shuttle has been seized by the Tektites, a group of rebel pirates . . .

. . . and the adventures begin!

Order a copy of this thrilling adventure here:

https://www.hiraethsffh.com/product-page/pyra-and-the-tektites-1-by-tyree-campbell

Adopted Child

By Teri Santitoro

Imp, now 13, has awakened from stasis by MA, the ship's computer, to find that everyone else has been killed by a highly infectious disease. She is alone on the ship. But she is about to have visitors.

The *Greentown*, a salvage ship, has spotted a derelict and is about to board her for salvage rights. The crew is blissfully unaware of what happened to the people on the derelict. Soon enough they will find out...but will it be too late? And what of the girl who now controls the derelict?

To everyone involved, everything is new... and potentially lethal.

Ordering Link:

https://www.hiraethsffh.com/product-page/adopted-child-by-t-santitoro

A Halloween Murder
David Aronlee
Illustration by Michelle St. James

There are two types of people. Those who close the closet doors to hide clutter and those who fear what might come out at night if they didn't.

Jake saw the small scattered peanut shells by the path leading from the front of his house. But he didn't pay much attention to them as he scrambled to catch the school bus just as it pulled up to the stop by the old oak tree. At school that day there was a lunchtime presentation on the Halloween cookie sale. He sat with his best friends: Tommy and Lizzy. Tommy could draw super cool pictures of monsters and gladiators, run faster than any other boy in his class, and had a bowl cut which Jake admired greatly. Lizzy had a long blond braid, could run as fast as Tommy, and could spit farther than any of them, which Jake also admired greatly.

The Halloween cookie presentation was all about the prizes they could each earn. Every prize was a monster that could protect the house on Halloween evening. For every fifty dollars of cookies sold, they could choose a bat dangling on a string with eyes that would light up at any movement. For one-hundred dollars they could each earn a large plastic spider and an accompanying web as big as Jake's comforter at home. Then they wheeled out the grand prize. The kid who sold the most cookies would win a full-size, animatronic werewolf, that would move, howl, and light up. Jake shied back a little in his seat at this, but the buzz in the cafeteria raised the volume level considerably as every kid considered winning that beautiful scary beast.

"I'm going to go for an army of bats," said Tommy.

"I want that blow up ghost in the tree," said Lizzy, eyeing the massive four-hundred-dollar ghost gripping the severed head of a pumpkin man. Jake knew Lizzy's family went for a phantasmagorical defense, with dozens of different types of ghosts: ghosts climbing trees, ghosts emerging from cauldrons, ghosts holding heads of skeletons and pumpkin-men. Tommy's family went more creature heavy, with huge gargoyles peering down from rain gutters as if they were battlements, and massive spiders and skeletons strewn between webs and tombstones in the yard. Before Jake could add what he had his eye on, Tommy spoke again.

"I feel bad for whoever doesn't get their house properly decorated before the fright-fest," said Tommy. "Can you imagine? Waking up in the middle of the night to claws..."

"Yeah," said Jake, with a sinking feeling. His family had just moved to town a few months earlier, and he had gone with his parents to the department store to pick up their new fridge when they realized the landlord didn't provide one in their house. He'd held his little brother's hand and seen his parents casting wistful glances at the Halloween decorations. He'd seen how expensive they were.

"Or a possession?" said Lizzy, getting excited, before noticing Jakes downcast eyes.

"Or a witch grabbing you and hauling you screaming onto her broomstick..." said Tommy. Lizzy kicked Tommy at this point and nodded at Jake who was staring at the ground.

"What?!" said Tommy. "Oh."

"Why don't you think the government just provides for monster protection for everyone," said Lizzy.

"Too expensive," says Tommy. "Besides, everyone knows what's coming on Halloween. Everyone knows you have to get your monster defenses up so when the portals between the worlds opens your house is safe. There's plenty of time to prepare."

"But it doesn't seem fair," said Lizzy.

Yeah, thought Jake silently.

"That's why so few people move," said Tommy. "It's not just the 'trest' rates."

"What does that mean?" asked Lizzy.

"You haven't heard about the 'trest rates?" said Tommy. "My dad was just talking about them. Something about money. Anyway, that's why you just have to be careful not to move right before Halloween..."

Jake thought about how his dad had gotten sick and lost his job and how they had to pay for his care from the Halloween emergency fund, and then move again so his mom could find another job. His parents hadn't told him any of that, but he'd noticed.

Their discussion subsided, but Jake resolved then and there to sell so many cookies he could come home with an army of bats, and ghosts, and that big werewolf, and show them all to his parents so that his little brother and parents would be safe this Halloween.

But after they all got their order forms and took the bus home, the crisp fall air swirling through the open windows, Jake realized how hard that would be. He went from house to house, but he didn't know the neighbors well yet. Most of the houses he knew had kids from his school who were also selling cookies. Most of the houses without kids had already stocked up on Halloween candy for the trick or treating that would go on before the sun set--everyone knew that earned Halloween candy was a little extra protection against the marauding spirits and beasts that would come out after sunset-- and didn't need any extra sugar.

"Thanks, but we are all set."

"No thanks."

"No, get lost kid."

With each house and each failure, the pit in the bottom of Jake's stomach grew and grew until he felt like it would swallow him whole. Which would be just like getting swallowed by some demon on Halloween because he hadn't been able to sell any cookies to help protect his house. Each morning he looked forlornly back at the largely unadorned façade of his family's little rental house, just a couple of carved pumpkins at the door, and his guilt grew.

By the time the day came to turn in the cookie order forms at school, the day before Halloween, Jake was so nervous he threw up in the boy's bathroom. Tommy took home nine bats. Lizzy didn't take home anything. She said her parents hadn't been interested in buying any cookies, they felt she was going to get enough sugar, so she had given up on that. She got Tommy to admit that all the cookies he sold had been to his parents and a couple aunts and uncles and that deflated his head a little bit.

Jake took home one dangling bat that day. He gave it to his mom and then went to his room and cried. He had failed and his family home would be destroyed. His little brother eaten. He thought of their old apartment. The building managers always took care of the decorations, it was part of the rent and one of the advantages in living in an apartment building. They had just needed a couple pumpkins in front of the door and some earned Halloween candy and the monsters had given them a wide birth. But this year would be different. His parents didn't have money for Halloween decorations, and he, Jake, the oldest, had failed to bring any meaningful protection home from school. Just one measly bat that would get overwhelmed by the first goblin to come by.

The next day he got dressed up to go trick-or-treating with Tommy and Lizzy. He wore a homemade mummy outfit: a roll of toilet paper borrowed from the school bathroom held together on him with some scotch-tape; and a few splashes of ketchup as the dried blood of his victims around the mouth and hands. Jake knew how important it was for trick-or-treating kids to have realistic costumes in case they were caught out after dark and had to blend in, or on the off chance an ambitious monster appeared before the sun had truly set. Lizzy showed up as the "ghost of the patriarchy" and

Tommy had decided to be a zombie with extremely undead-like face-paint his mom did for him. Jake sighed inwardly, but was comforted they didn't ask him where he got the toilet paper from.

Jake stayed out as late as he could. First Lizzy, then Tommy, went home as the sun got low, each warning him to get home before the sun set entirely and the monsters started coming out. But Jake knew he needed as much earned Halloween candy as he could possibly get. Finally, after three houses in a row that didn't open the door for him, he turned for home. At first he shuffled slowly, trying to blend in, ignoring the glowing eyes in the bushes on the side of the road that were beginning to blink open. Then he felt a gentle cold tingle on the back of his neck and crossed his fingers and imagined sunshine. He didn't look up when a shadow swooped by, but when he turned onto his street and heard a loud cackle from a witch whooshing overhead his resolve broke and he sprinted, chanting the rhyme his mother taught him when he was younger: "Halloween, no monsters near, eat some candy and have no fear."

He made it home and slammed the door behind him even as he heard skittering in the road coming after him. He had flown up the driveway and past the makeshift ghost cutouts and bats his younger brother had done in art class, past his one bat and their three pumpkins. His parents hugged him close, half-scolding him, half crying that he had stayed out so late and risked so much for a little extra candy.

He put his candy on the table and let his mom lead him to bed. He fully expected to be woken in the middle of the night to a living nightmare inside the house. And he knew it would be all his fault. He tossed and turned, listening to the howling and the shrieks and moans and screams coming through the window as all the monsters of the spirit realm marauded. At one point, as the screams got louder he decided he'd rather see what was coming and crept softly out of bed, so as not to wake his younger brother, and peeked through the blinds. He spotted glowing eyes and heard howls and hisses and saw, in the light of the lone street lamp at the end of the driveway, a hunt of vampires collide with a mischief of huge trolls. There was a massive thump as a bloody stump of an arm was flung against his window and he cried out and leapt back into bed, fully expecting the window to shatter at any moment. But it held and the screams passed and his brother just let out a whimper and rolled over. Finally, Jake slept.

When he woke up the next morning it was quiet. So quiet, he thought maybe he was dead. He turned over and his little brother was gone and he had a moment of panic, imagining giant tentacles coming through the window to grab his little brother in the night, when he heard laughter from the kitchen. He went out and his whole family was there, eating bat shaped pancakes.

He just said, "but how?" His dad, understanding his question, just winked and took his hand and led him outside. He didn't see any additional decorations at first.

"Look on the roof," his dad said. He looked up and lined all along the roof were crows. Dozens of them.

"A murder of crows," said his dad. "They kept watch over us. Nature provides the best defense on Halloween."

"But how..." said Jake again.

"Your mother and I have been putting up peanuts on the roof for them every morning. They've become our good friends, and returned the favor for us last night, watching over us."

Jake just shook his head in awe. "A murder. Of crows." Then he went back inside and had pancakes.

The Hungry Vampire in Space
Gary Davis

How does a vampire travel through space?
Not on a rocket; that won't go far.

Downsize to a cosmic dust speck.
Then hitch a laser beam to a star.

What if you get a ravenous urge?
Outer space is always sheer night.

Not to worry, your food is right there.
Take a bite of your beam—the blood is the light!

Mellie

The Adventures of a Teenage Vampire

Meet Mellie, an adolescent vampire, as she travels to Italy and New York to discover roots, make friends, and of course get into trouble. Fun adventures for the whole family.

https://www.hiraethsffh.com/product-page/mellie-the-adventures-of-a-teenage-vampire-by-debby-feo

The Other World
Cheryl J. Brown

Tage gripped his space suit and slid it on Monday morning. His space helmet was where he always kept it, on his bedside table, next to the window that gave him a full view of the Mars Command Space Academy.

If it wasn't summer vacation he would have been in there on the top floor learning about space travel or time dimension, or knee deep in pens and pads and artifacts in one of those other classrooms learning about space, exploration, and the solar system.

He stared at the twelve level structure, made of iron and shiny metal, that almost clipped the top of the biodome. **Mars Colonized 2200** the sign read in gold letters. Tage liked reading the sign before bed. The blue streetlights made it look powerful.

He was proud to have the view, but still…if he could change the view he would.

Other kids in the biodomes lived in the nearby colonies. Their bedroom views consisted of downtown Mars with all the large, triangular buildings that shined like chrome and the hover cars and electro scooters that zoomed by in the air.

He envied those kids for having that awesome view. All he got was an angled view of their school at all times. He rolled his astute eyes. "Figures, the grandson of one of the founding fathers of Mars would live on the command base."

There was a light rapping on his door and his dad poked his head in, "Good morning, son." At all times, his dad sported a white lab coat, high pants with suspenders, wire-rim glasses, and crazy hair. He looked like a scientist- *"a good one at that."* His dad always added cheerfully. "Ready for your trip? Today's a great day to blast off."

Tage grew tired of that joke very quickly, considering how often he traveled back and forth to Earth, but he managed to chuckled at his humorless, one-liner, "Sure, dad. Blast away to space."

"That's the spirit. I have breakfast ready for you. Sorry, no sugar or fruit for the oatmeal, but there's nothing wrong with a little bland oatmeal. Am I right? Huh?"

"No worries, dad. I'm not hungry." He was hungry but he refused to eat bland oatmeal. "And besides with the way I handle my spaceship I'll be on Earth in time for lunch."

"Good, son. Follow me."

Tage followed his dad through their little apartment. Attached to the far right of their balcony was the walkway to The Mars Command Center. It was a quarter of a mile and solid glass. They passed familiar scientist, data experts, and busy employees who sipped from white, styrofoam cups and carried armfuls of papers. Those guys always seemed to be in a rush, Tage thought.

His father slipped his arm around his shoulders and squeezed, "Your journey should be easy, son. Rudimental. No wayward space rocks, ice chunks, or meteoroids are detected in your route as far as we can see. Though..."

"What is it, dad?"

"A spacecraft to Saturn, one of those touring space cruises, hit warp speed last night."

"What's the big deal? There's a million of those flying all over this solar system and hitting warp speed."

"I know but the captain wasn't paying attention and he came too close to Venus's atmosphere and he hit warp speed there. It stirred up some toxic, acidic gases. We monitored the after effect and feared an unstable disturbance would materialize."

"Did it?" He asked curiously.

"No, from what we monitored, everything appears fine. There is however a long range of orange and pink gas hovering the area. Most of it has dissipated. Nothing but some residual heated gas particles still floating, I suppose. But be careful, son. You know how to handle your spaceship well. You'll be fine."

Once Tage was secure and locked into his spaceship his dad messaged him over the radio, "Tell your mother I said hello."

"Will do, dad."

His parents were divorced. His mother lived on Earth while his dad moved to Mars to be closer to his job at the command center. From an early age, he traveled to both locations to see his parents. He preferred Mars and lived there mostly, but his mother always had him during summer vacations and special holidays.

With the flick of several dials and the signal to proceed from the command center he counted down from ten and launched into space. The current arrival time was one p.m. He always liked to push his spacecraft to beat the expected time. He turned on warp speed and hit the cruise control button. He had close to five hours until his destination. He promptly picked out a comic book from under his dashboard, propped up his heels, and began to read quietly.

Around noon, Tage entered Venus's realm. The noxious orange and pink gases his dad warmed him about were still present and much larger than he anticipated. Once he entered it there was turbulence and a bright, neon glow erupted as he traveled through the formation, but once he exited it, it was smooth space flying.

The rest of the trip was uneventful, but passing through the mass disrupted Tage's radio and the communication to both Mars's and Earth's command centers were lost. For an hour, he fiddled with the dials and called to both bases with no luck. There was no static or garbling noise just dead silence.

When he finally started to descend towards Earth and broke through its clouds in the troposphere he knew instantly something was wrong. Where the command center should have been with its expansive buildings and parking lots was nothing more than tall grass- an open field of nothingness that spread into the countryside for miles.

He checked his coordinates to make sure his landing point was correct and wasn't skewed, but everything was in order. He was baffled. Where was the command center? He flew over miles of green land, empty embankments, and hills. All the while, his GPS notified him he passed his destination point.

After twenty minutes, he finally stumbled across a small town in the distance. On the outskirts of it he landed his spaceship near a small grove of trees and a dense muddled pond. He followed the highway for half a mile and saw an outdated brick building with the words: HOME DINER on its opaque window and he walked in.

Patrons were in the diner and all of them stopped eating and looked at him curiously. He unsnapped his helmet and looked at them. They all looked odd and dated from their hairstyles to their fashion. The old man who wiped the counter near the register said, "Hiya, kid, what did you do? Leave a party?" He laughed, "Have a seat and order something. Cold root beer float for you?"

He ignored the curious eyes on him and went to the man, "Sir, where am I? I missed the command center. My coordinates are functioning fine but it still reads I passed it. I had to travel twenty minutes to get here."

"Command center? You really are playing your part with the act, Kid. I can tell you're not from around here based on your accent. I'm sure your parents are somewhere around here lost as well, just tell them they're in Cypress, California. Got it?"

"I've never heard of Cypress. Where is Treadway? That's where The National Command Center is located."

The man sighed, "Kid, enough games, already. I have to get back to work, if you want to order, go ahead. There is no Treadway or National Command Center around here. This is just a quiet little town in the middle of nowhere."

A woman resting on a nearby barstool dressed in an odd polk-a-dot dress and a weird, pinned up hairstyle finished her drink and slid the paper she was reading to the side. She thanked the man and slid him a coin across the counter and scooted by him and the doorbell chimed on the way out.

Tage was utterly confused. He didn't understand what was going on. Perhaps the odd town full of strange people was just a misdirection on his part. Still, perhaps the paper the woman left could give him some insight. He walked over, put his helmet on the stool, and picked it up.

Written in bold, cursive letters it read the **Cypress Review**. Underneath it was some minor national news about the Soviet Union and other European countries that signed the Warsaw Pact last week. Soviet Union? Warsaw Pact? He thought curiously, the names sounded familiar but he could have sworn he remembered hearing about that in American History class and its timing being before the twenty-first century.

He skimmed over car shows, grocery sales, local awards, and he found the date written in the top right corner. May 17th 1955. No, that was wrong he thought. Today was May 17th 2260.

"Why is this paper here?" He asked the man who was now refilling coffee orders.

"That's the latest paper, hot off the press. Anyone can read it at their leisure."

"What's today's date?"

"May 17th."

"The year, sir, the year." He implored.

"1955. What did you do, kid? Fall and hit your head before you put on that space suit? You are acting mighty strange."

"That's impossible. It's not 1955. It's 2260. I'm from Mars and I've come to spend the summer with-"

The entire diner laughed. He looked around them angrily as he shouted, "The year is 2260! I'm from Mars! My address is-"

"Kid, enough shenanigans," The man rubbed his ample belly and chuckled, "Get out of here. No more jokes. You're causing a disruption. Go on."

He grabbed his helmet and charged out the diner. He ran and got away from the strange town as fast as he could. He got to his spaceship and climbed in. He checked his gauges and he had enough fuel to make it back to Mars, and that's what he intended to do.

He hit warp speed and flew through space at an astronomical rate. When he came to Venus the orange and pink formation was still there. As soon as he exited it the monitors and controls on his dashboard started to squawk and squeak. He fiddled with the controls and found a weak signal, "Mars base, this is Tage. Respond back!"

He heard gurgling and low mumbles, and couldn't quite make out what he heard. He fiddled with the dials for hours but couldn't get anyone. Once he descended back to the landing docket and landed his ship his father and several of the scientist came charging out.

He jumped out, threw his helmet to the side, and ran towards his dad. "Son, am I glad you're here! Are you alright? We lost communication with you." He hugged him.

After he caught his breath he stumbled over his words, "Da-dad, it was- was. I don't know. It was so peculiar. I-I those people were-"

"Shh, son. Catch your breath. Don't talk. What's this?" He took the newspaper out of his hand and read it. "What is this?"

"I found it at a diner." He explained, "When I was going to land, Earth's base wasn't there. Nothing but miles of fields and green hills. I landed near a town and walked to a diner. Inside, the people were so odd and dressed strange. They never heard of The National Command Center or Treadway and the town I was in I never heard of. I read that paper while I was there. But dad, no one believed I was from Mars! They thought I was joking. They all laughed at me and looked at me like I was crazy!"

"This doesn't make sense. This paper is dated for over three hundred years." He passed the paper around so his fellow co-workers could glance at it.

His dad dropped to his level and gripped his shoulders, "Son, it's possible that you were transferred to another time period. There's no wonder these people looked strange. Time travel and time jumping is physically possible but we haven't narrowed down the science of it yet. Was there anything different about your trip? Anything that you can share with us? You did loose communication for a selected part of time?"

Tage thought about it, "I only lost communication when I went through that formation near Venus."

"The orange and pink gases!" Someone shouted.

"I knew there was something different about it!" Someone else agreed.

"Tage, my boy, you just discovered something monumental! You slipped through a time portal and traveled into the past. And we have the proof!" He held up the newspaper and looked around them, "By are calculations the mass is not spreading or vaporizing but staying a consistent size. We should began running test now and we should send someone else through the portal to collect data. Gentlemen, what are we waiting for? Someone get one of those spaceships started, someone call the earth's command center," and his dad continued to shout orders.

His dad kissed his forehead, "You just unlocked valuable keys of the universe and the mechanics of it. You'll be iconic just like your grandfather." He grabbed Tage and cheered, "Let's go son, we have to let the science community know our discovery and you have to give your initial report. You, Tage, are going to go down in history as the first person to ever time travel."

Pointy Things
Adele Gardner

I don't need a conical witch's hat.
I have the exclamation point of my black tail,
a weathervane warning of dangers.
I boast the perfect points of two furry black ears,
which prick at the eerie hoot of the great horned owl
who hunts for cats each night,
extended talons ready to strike.
There's a pecking order among Halloween creatures,
and he's jealous of my magic,
of my eighteen diamond-sharp claws
when he has only eight.
Yes, he has wings, but soon I'll be
yowling across the moon, as light as air,
surfing on neat straw bristles
behind my laughing witch,
our pointed broom
guiding us through the dangers and magic
of another glorious Halloween night,
sharp with autumn's chill.

The Adventures of Colo Collins & Tama Toledo in Space and Time
By Tyree Campbell

Out on their first date, high school seniors Colo Collins and Tama Toledo are invited aboard a spaceship and offered the chance to intervene in various events in the Universe. These events can range from stopping an asteroid from striking a planet to helping someone find her house keys. But there's a catch: both Colo and Tama have to agree that an intervention should be performed . . . and sometimes they'll have to perform the intervention themselves!

Ordering Link:

https://www.hiraethsffh.com/product-page/adventures-of-colo-collins-tama-toledo-in-space-and-time-by-tyree-campbell

A Graveyard Promise
Drew Alexander Ross
Illustration by Michelle St. James

The graveyard existed since the days of the first settlers. Other burial grounds might have been there before, but I never knew. Regardless, the touch of death and spirit were always there.

When I was a child, the graveyard was on the edge of town. The hallowed grounds were on a hill by the church, looking out at the bay. The smith's daughter and I would sneak past the rectory to sit on the hill and take in the brilliant colors of sunset as they faded into the darkness of the night. We made a promise the last night she watched the moon rise over that hill.

The promise was never fulfilled.

***

The graveyard receded into the background as time went on. The residents of the town ceased to bury their dead there. I never bothered to see where they made their new boneyard. I watched on as the mourners became fewer and fewer, and people stopped paying their respects. Firs and Black Gum trees crept in, along with the brush. A cart path went through the middle of the hill where the oldest markers once told who walked before them.

Now, the road was crumbled rock paved smooth. A stone wall at the road's edge kept the rest of the hill and the past away from those traveling by. A new church was built upon the grounds where the old one resided. Woods grew in and separated the graveyard from the place of worship. The only people who walked the hallowed ground now were the children who disrespected the dead and sought the truth to the rumors of an old village tale.

I made sure they didn't leave disappointed. And I made sure they didn't come back.

***

The leaves began to change colors. It was approaching the time of year when I might come across a few children interested in a nighttime stroll through the graveyard. In recent years, children seemed to enjoy their visits to the cemetery, often causing a stir. In times past, there would have been reverence when walking among the dead.

The children of these times, with hair obscuring their vision or stuck up with some kind of grease, would call out to the spirits with bravado. Their courage disappeared when I responded.

I sat on my marker, an unreadable withered stone, and stared out at the waves of the bay glittering in the moonlight. The light that shone out over the water and through the trees shone through me.

A fallen branch cracked and alerted me to the presence of an outsider in the graveyard. I made my translucent form invisible and followed a young girl's progression through the cemetery.

The girl couldn't have been much older than 11. Her body hadn't yet caught up to her gangly limbs. She didn't have the clown-like makeup I'd seen other young girls of the century sport. She wore tan pants that cut above her knees, a baggy garment as a top, and wore white shoes. Her dirt-blonde hair was tied back, but she also had hair cut short that hung across her forehead. A silver chain around her neck glimmered in the moonlight.

The girl peered around the graveyard and sat next to my gravestone. She looked out at the bay and sighed. My insides, at least what I felt of them, coiled, and my temper flared. This girl dared to encroach on my hallowed grounds.

But I had a remedy for her infection of my space.

I moved silently. I could have been a touch of the wind as I drifted beside her and lowered my head.

"Boo!"

The girl bristled and sat up straight.

"If you think I'm scared of some stupid boy trying to frighten me, you're wrong!"

I took an involuntary step back. I rarely encountered defiance from a human since I decided to haunt the graveyard. And never from a little girl.

The girl scoffed and turned her head, "Too scared to show your face because your trick didn't work?"

I grinned. I knew the perfect response to her verbal jab.

I took to my translucent form as she stared right in my direction. Her eyes widened, and I snarled.

I waited for her to scream, ready to unleash my cackle of laughter as she fled the hill. But after a sharp intake of breath, she leaned forward and stared at me.

Again, I was speechless.

"Why are you trying to scare me?"

A sour taste of a not-quite-ripe berry filled my mouth. *How dare she question the dead.*

"What do you think I would do? You are trespassing in a land meant for the dead! It belongs to no living soul."

"I'm not bothering you."

"Your very presence bothers me."

"Well, that's your problem."

After she told me off, she promptly turned her head back to the water and ignored me.

A numbing cold, like death, settled over me as I realized there was nothing more I could do to frighten this girl. I turned myself invisible and sulked back amongst the trees. My tactics hadn't worked... I never needed any others...

I watched until she left an hour later. A slight twinge of satisfaction filled me as I watched her go. But the pang of excitement became more like a cold pulse, like a prick from a winter thorn. I wanted to enjoy the moment of her retreat fully, and I didn't understand why I couldn't.

***

I stalked the graveyard each night, waiting for her return. About a week passed before the girl visited again. This time, I knew how I would deal with her.

"Begone from this place! Any who dwell among the dead while their hearts still beat will be cursed!"

"Oh, be quiet," the girl said as she marched up the hill.

The girl caught sight of me as she marched up toward my grave. I felt a burning sensation in my cheeks as the corner of her lips curled upwards in a small smile.

"Why aren't you afraid of me!"

The girl sat beside my grave again, "If you could have done something, you would have done it last time."

I drifted back toward the trees, feeling as hollow as I did in those first days of death. The feeling of uselessness I had tried so hard to forget returned fresh. If I had bothered to turn back, I would have seen the girl's sadness reflected in her downward look and glazed eyes.

Instead, I disappeared into the night.

***

Another week passed before I was disturbed from sulking by voices in the dark. I cast my gaze away but couldn't stop from glancing back at the figure that came up the hill.

"Shouldn't she be here?"

"We'll find her. And she'll regret what she said."

A smaller figure with carrot-colored hair stormed away from a larger raven-haired figure and cast her gaze around the graveyard. They both wore uniforms that seemed to belong to the military of some foreign nation. Badges decorated a sash over their shirts.

"Where is she?" the small girl with red hair quipped. "The meeting was over ages ago."

"She might be hiding," the large, dark-haired girl responded.

"Well, let's make her come out and play."

The malice of the small one's words worried me.

The blonde-haired girl wasn't by my grave. If she was coming tonight, she should have been here by now. But maybe she was just late. If so, it would not be good for her to happen upon the current situation. The military girls didn't seem alike to the other.

I smiled to myself. That thought gave me an idea.

"What was that?"

"What was what?" the redhead replied.

A gust of wind blew leaves, dirt, and twigs at the girls' faces. They raised their arms to protect themselves. The red-haired girl glanced around the graveyard. She set her eyes on a gravestone a few meters away.

"I think I've found her."

I glanced behind me and saw a white shoe retreat behind an old headstone. I then turned back to the two approaching girls and raised my invisible arms. The wind was drawn through me and rushed toward the girls, forcing them back a step.

"Let's go," her friend implored. "I don't like this!"

"Stupid wind!" the redhead called out.

I took my cue.

"What if it's not the wind..."

The girls glanced at each other and turned back toward my gravestone. I appeared with a snarl. Their wide-eyed fear changed to fully dilated panic.

They screamed and ran down the hill back toward the church. Their screams faded like the dying wind.

I smiled and turned back to see the blonde-haired girl standing up from behind the gravestone a few meters from mine. She had tears in her eyes.

"Why did they want to harm you?"

She shrugged, "Why do you want to frighten people who come to the graveyard?"

I sighed and cast my eyes to the ground. My chest felt like a weight was dragged through it down to my stomach. I did not like to think about the answer to her question. That was why I avoided the question over the years until it became a habit to forget. To confront it again would be to address my fears and those past regrets.

"Well?" the girl asked, wiping away her tears.

My eyes found the girl's. I had thought I was strong by ignoring the past and avoiding my emotions. But summoning up the courage to face the girl and her question, I realized I was not strong before. I was just a scared boy who had died ages ago.

***

I told the blonde-haired girl of the promise I made to another on the hill long ago. On the last night the smith's daughter and I saw the moonlight together, I promised my love would protect her, follow her ship back to England, and be with her when she returned. But I couldn't fulfill that promise. I died shortly after she left... And I decided to wait.

I never saw or heard of the smith's daughter again. And in death, I dwelled in the depression of not being able to do anything about it. So, I stopped remembering. But the pain was still there. I never knew if my love was able to protect her.

"You protected me tonight."

I started at the blonde-haired girl. She smiled and nodded her head.

Warmth spread through my body in a way I hadn't felt since I had been alive. My form began to fade with the realization of the promise being honored. I had the choice again to move on. But I couldn't leave yet.

"Are you going to confront those girls?

"Are you joking? The tall one could stomp me like a bug. And the little one is more ferocious than a cat!"

"Not all monsters need to be fought. Just faced."

The girl's gaze dropped.

"They're mad because I'm not going to their slumber parties anymore. And I called them the oaf princess and annoying pea in front of our Girl Scout troop."

I didn't understand most of what she said, but I felt she was avoiding something.

"Why are you coming to the graveyard instead of the slumber parties?"

The girl touched the silver chain that hung around her neck.

"My grandpa died..." she said. "I don't feel like being around other people that are so happy."

"I understand... But your time for the graveyard should be a long way away. And you shouldn't be alone."

The girl stared at the ground, "What should I do?"

"You said you didn't want to be around people that were so happy. They didn't look happy to me... Maybe you can tell the girls what you're going through... Maybe you can help each other... And if not, at least you won't be hiding anymore."

The girl kept her head down for a while. Finally, she let out a long sigh and nodded. She turned to peer out at the bay. I joined her, and we stood for a time in peace.

"What about you?" She asked. "Are you going to haunt this graveyard forever?"

I took a moment before I responded, "I think I can finally move on."

"Good," she responded. "I don't like you being here all alone."

"Well, I promise to move on if you do."

"It's a promise," she smiled and touched my hand.

For the briefest moment, I felt something. Then, the girl turned and marched back toward the church. We both melted into the darkness.

The Caves of Titan
By Debby Feo

Students at the Galileo Interplanetary School explore new-found caves on Titan, where they encounter the Cenote People and learn to get along with them—and with each other, as they continue to grow and learn in a diverse student body. Still, there are conflicts to resolve . . . and some of them might put an end to the school!

https://www.hiraethsffh.com/product-page/caves-of-titan-by-debby-feo

Little Ghost
Margaret Zotkiewicz

As Little Ghost's sisters got dressed for
    the ball,
Held in the attic the first night of fall.
Little Ghost scurried and scampered and hid
She could not dance like her big sisters did!

They flitted and floated and fussed with
    their bows,
They dipped and soared and sank and rose.
Big Sister swirled and swiveled in lace,
While Mid Sister dashed like a horse in a race.

Little Ghost shivered and trembled in fear,
"Please, may I wait to attend next year?
I cannot boogie or shimmy or shake.
What kind of dancing ghost will I make?"

"Rise up Little Ghost and follow our groove,
Your sisters will show you just how to move."
They grabbed Little Ghost with a swish and
    a twirl,
and raced toward the steps with their skirts
    all awhirl.

Little Ghost slunk to the corner and cried.
"I cannot dance, I've tried and tried!"
"You'll do just fine," Big Sister said.
She suddenly shrank to the floor in dread.

"Look out, Little Ghost, it's Mean Tom the cat,
Ready to chase the Scary Black Bat!
Mean Tom is nasty and dirty and smelly,
He turns all the ghosts into bowls full of jelly."

Little Ghost scuttled and scampered and
    swayed,
"Oh no Sister Ghosts do not be afraid.
Mean Tom isn't mean, he's far from that,
He's just an old softie, a silly housecat!"

Little Ghost shuffled and ruffled Tom's fur,
And Mean Tom pranced up the steps with
    a purr.
Then Little Ghost circled round Scary Black
    Bat,
Who flew out the window past Mean Tom
    the cat.

Little Ghost shimmied and shook and giggled,
She flew to the attic with a laughing-fit wiggle.
"Come on Sister Ghosts, we cannot be late,
The First Night Ball simply cannot wait!"

Big Sister lifted and lofted and twittered,
As Mid Sister flashed and fluttered and
skittered.
"Little Ghost, Star of the First Night Ball,
You're the best dancing ghost of all!

Near and Far
Laurel Hanson

A bagful of popcorn kernels, three ripe tomatoes, three wire coat hangers, and six marbles. That's all it's going to take for me to be able to see without glasses. I am super nearsighted and have to wear these really thick glasses that I hate. I've been wearing them since I was eight and thought the bright pink frames were awesome. But now I'm eleven and they are not remotely awesome. My folks can't afford new frames, so I have to take this chance.

I know it's ridiculous, but I don't care.

Here's the thing. My dad had sent me out to check our upper field for whatever was beating paths in the hay along the border.

Well, I found it.

It was a little bigger than me and looked sort of like the caterpillar in *Alice in Wonderland*, if the caterpillar wore a velvet vest trimmed with sparkly pockets all down the front. It was sticking all its different hands into the different pockets and pulling things out. Or putting things in. I couldn't quite tell because its hands moved super-fast. Pebbles, pieces of hay, tiny three-fingered fistfuls of dirt, a bottle cap, and more shot into, or out of, the pockets. The caterpillar thing was humming to itself as it worked, kind of a nasal whizzing.

I probably should have gone to get dad, but he's been saying lately that I'm 'old enough now to do more work around the farm,' so I can't go running to him every time anything weird happens. Like when I find a giant caterpillar thing in the hay.

I circled it to see if it was maybe a kid in a costume or some kind of robotic toy. There was no zipper or antenna or anything that might explain it. I'd guess it was an escapee from a book, but that would be crazy.

"What are you?" I asked.

It whipped what might have been its head around. Tendrils sticking out the top zeroed in on my location. It squeaked out, "Yeeksi day!" and slapped a couple of its hands on its chest like my great Aunt Jane faking a heart attack. But it didn't spit acid at me or make any threatening movements, so I decided to try to negotiate, which I figured is what a big kid might do.

"You're ruining the hay fields."

It reared back, hands patting its pockets as if it thought I was going to steal from it. We had a little staring contest while the sun beat down between us and some crows scolded us for being in their territory.

Finally, it started talking from a mouth on the top of its head. "Don't worry about it, little boy. I'll fix it."

I wasn't all that surprised when it spoke since it was wearing the vest thing and, in books, animals in clothes usually talk. But I still didn't know what it was. Alien? Mutant?

"How can you fix the field? You've, like, trompled paths all over half an acre. Anyway, I'm a girl."

"Yeeksi! Last time I visited, girls put themselves into big pockets with the bottoms cut out."

I figured it meant 'dresses' but didn't bother to correct it. I liked the idea of putting myself in a pocket, but that wasn't the important thing. "So you've been here before?"

"A little piece of a long time ago. When I was..." it held some of the hands to its middle section to indicate how tall it had been.

"Did you eat up all the hay then, too?"

"There wasn't hay here then and anyway, I'm not eating it. I need it for... construction purposes."

"What are you making?"

"That's on a need-to-know basis."

"Where are you from?"

"Near and far. Near and far."

"How can that be? That's like opposites at the same time."

"Exactly!" it said, the way you'd say, 'who's a good boy?' to a puppy.

"That doesn't make any sense."

Three of the balloon-shaped sections in its middle filled up and then expelled air. "It's a matter of perspective. Far in space, right around the corner in distance."

"That makes less sense. Distance moves through space." I knew that at least.

"You think that about time as well, no doubt."

"You're a time traveler? That is so cool! Wait, are you what humans will look like in the future?"

It blinked several of the eyes on the ends of the tendrils. "Don't be silly. I could not have evolved from a bi-pedal, warm-blooded article such as yourself." It sniffed and took a scrap of cloth out of a pocket to blot at what I thought might be its nose. Or belly button.

"So, *are* you a time traveler?"

"In a way, in a way." Its arms rippled down its sides. "Time, being as it is less forward than humans take it to be, means distance is less far than humans take it to be."

"You are just messing with me."

"Maybe. Or maybe the truth is hard to see." It pulled some dirt out of its pocket and tossed it into its mouth like trail mix.

I wondered if the vest was some kind of alien protective gear, like a space suit that helped it process our air and water. So I asked it.

"This garment is high fashion!" It sounded insulted.

I thought I should be more direct. "Are you an alien?"

It looked even more offended. "Alien, indeed!" It clapped one of its hands on its head in what must be a universal sign for 'stupid.' Then it added, "You might say I am a next-door neighbor of alternate being."

I was beginning to think I was hallucinating. I took off my glasses to clean them, squinting at his now fuzzy shape.

"What is that?" the not-alien-but-alternate-being-maybe-hallucination asked. "Without those orbs can you not see me?" It sounded hopeful.

"No, I can still see you, but I can see you better with them. They're called glasses."

"Ah well that explains that then," it muttered.

"Explains what?"

"I wondered if I was stuck inter-dimensionally or if you had some magic apparatus allowing you to cross over the barriers. It would appear the former, not the later, is the case."

"I don't know what you're saying."

"All for the best, all for the best."

"Anyway, I'm supposed to get rid of you because you're damaging the field."

"You need only ask, and I shall be gone."

And it literally turned on the spot and began to trot away. I trotted next to it, and as it picked up speed, I did too. I was barely hurrying. With its little legs, it couldn't take very big steps. This seemed to upset it, and it tried for a burst of speed like a marathoner in the final stretch, only the final stretch was the edge of the field where the forest meets the hay in a thick tangle of undergrowth which snagged it like a fly in a web.

It began to make piercing sounds of distress, throwing in some English words like "Drat!" and "Piffle!" and "Oh crumb cakes!" It seemed to like the last one a lot and repeated it a few times.

"Calm down, you're getting stuck even worse by flailing around like that. Those are burdocks."

It froze. "Am I being held hostage? I've heard this happens when humans want gold."

I had no idea what it was talking about. "No, it's just a plant. You have to be careful." I began pulling the burrs out of his velvet vest thing while it made weird noises like a chain saw trying to sing a nursery rhyme.

"My friends are going to be way impressed when I tell them about you," I said, trying to distract it.

"Oh no! You must not!"

"Why not? You're cool."

"I am, in fact, quite heated. Further, no one is to know that I have been here. Yourself excepted of course, and I expect you to keep mum about it."

"Why?" When it didn't answer, I plowed on. "Are you ashamed of what you are? Like are you a mutant? I mean, you shouldn't be. Ashamed that is. You should take pride in yourself and your differences."

The mutant blinked at me from the ends of several of its tendrils.

"Do not impugn my nature by referring to me as a mutant, you rude child."

"Well, what *are* you?"

"Just a neighbor having a little trouble unvisiting itself." Its many hands were plucking the spikey burrs out of its vest way faster than I could, and it popped one in its mouth. "Tasty!"

Yep, it ate the burdocks. Which are like spiky balls of irritation if you've never been in the woods. Or outside.

"Maybe my dad can help. He's good with tools and..."

"No!" All the hands came up at once and spiraled around, like it was doing the 'wax on, wax off' maneuver. "No one can know I am here. Even you."

"But I already know you're here.""A problem, yes. A conundrum, in fact. But an impossibility, no." It waved its eye tendrils at me. "Tell me, those glasses you wear. Does that mean you cannot see as is normal for your kind?"

"Yeah."

"I have a proposal." It leaned forward like my friend April does when she wants to tell a secret, even though none of her secrets are any good. Or even really secrets. "If you don't tell anyone I am here, I can fix your eyes."

"Get out of town!"

It blinked a couple of times. "That is what I am attempting to do."

"What I mean is you can't do that!"

"Why not?"

"Well, no one's been able to fix my eyes."

"I have certain abilities. You will see, provided..."

"...I don't tell anyone about you?"

"That is the heart of it, that is the nub."

"How do I know you won't blind me? You could be like one of those telemarketers making promises but totally lying."

It started waxing on, waxing off again. "I would not do such a thing to a creature who has done me no harm."

"Meaning if I harmed you, you could make me go blind?"

"That's on a need-to-know basis."

"And if you fix my eyes, and I don't tell anyone about you, you'll leave our fields?"

"That's the heart of it!" The creature flushed pea green, which is weird, but not as weird as all those hands waxing on and off. It took a little leather bag out of one of its pockets and handed it to me. "I will need that filled with popcorn--unpopped--three tomatoes, some wire, and I don't suppose you could produce any marbles?"

Which is what brings me to the point where I am running back through the field with a leather bag of popcorn kernels, three tomatoes, three wire coat hangers, and six of my brother's marbles.

I find the caterpillar laying by the burdock bushes with what looks like puke puddled up on the ground next to it. It hops up and takes all the stuff I brought, making happy chuckly noises. Stretching out the coat hangers, it lays them flat in a hoop around its feet with the ends sticking in the earth about one inch apart. He starts mashing the tomatoes into the gaps between the wire.

"How's all this going to get you back where you're supposed to be?"

"That's on a need-to-know basis."

"OK. Then can you fix my eyes before you go?" I take off my glasses and take a shaky breath because I'm not sure if it's going to blind me. Or worse. If there is such a thing.

It points most of its hands at the slimy puke puddle. "A little bit of that will do the job. Most likely."

"Yeah. No." I say.

It gives me a look like its the only one who can speak in contradictions. "Alright then," and then it leans over, sucks a loogie of the stuff up into one of its tendril things, and shoots it right into my eyes.

It splats all over my face. In my eyes, nose, mouth. I scream and start running around. "Gross! Gross! Gross!" I'm blinded by the goo, trying to swab it out with my fingers, but it's like slithery gum. I am beyond angry. What kind of practical joke is this?

I finally pull the last strands away from my face and wipe it with my shirttails. The caterpillar is standing there looking awful pleased with itself, even rocking back and forth a bit as if to say, "I told you so."

In fact, it then says, "I told you so."

"What? How could you do that? That is the most disgusting thing I have ever—I don't even know."

"And where are your glasses?"

I touch my face and remember that I took them off right before it shot me in the eyes. I see them lying in the dirt, winking pinkly up at me in the evening light. I look up and I can see across the grain to the roofs of the farmhouse and the barn and the silo. And the mountains beyond. Clear as anything.

I blink, rub my eyes, and stare again, because in my whole life, I've never been able to see this well.

"Is this permanent?" I ask.

"Inasmuch as you are not a permanent creature, no. But as long as the eyes are with you, then you should see like that."

"I don't understand how you did that."

"Sight is just a matter of perception."

"That makes no sense."

It shrugs, sending a ripple down its various arm sockets. "Be that as it may, you can see, so I'll toddle off now. Remember, mum's the word!"

It waves gaily, squishes the last tomato into place between the wires and pitches the marbles at me.

I duck as they ping into me, and when I look up, the caterpillar is gone. The air in the hoop is wavering like summer heat haze and I hear popcorn popping. "Delicious!" it shouts, and then it burps. But I cannot see it.

Picking up my glasses, I put them on, but they make the world fuzzy and I still don't see the caterpillar. I take them off, feeling my heart begin to swell as the world comes into focus, everything crisp and clear, both near and far. I feel like I did when I won the award at the talent show for my magic act. Only more. Way more.

I scan the field in case the caterpillar is hiding behind a tree or something, but I don't think it is. I think it's gone, leaving only a ring of wire on the ground and some sizzling tomatoes.

Feeling pretty pumped, I practically dance through the fields on my way home. Without my glasses I can see individual trees in the hills, the old combine in the next field, the pattern of the heads of grain waving in the wind. I can see everything!

The thing is, I start to see other things too. Things that *aren't* supposed to be there.

A flicker in the corner of my eye makes me twist my head around, but there's nothing there. Then I think I see a pointy red cone about two feet off the ground, but when I blink, it's gone. I spot little figures swaying on the stalks of hay, blurry and fast like dragonflies, but I would swear they have arms and legs.

I rub my eyes. I can still see everything clearly. It's just that I'm seeing all these other things clearly too. Things from fairy tale books that were supposed to stay in the books, not come out into our fields. But there they are, all around.

By the time I get back to the house, I've spotted a gnome, four pixies, a kind of troll thing, and some walking mushrooms that appeared to be having a parade. When I reached down to touch them, they freaked out and ran away.

"Near and far," the caterpillar had said. Near and far. All these creatures have been here all along, next-door neighbors, but also not here. Somewhere else far away.

And I can see them. It's confusing to have creatures that aren't really there popping in and out of my line of sight. When I step into the kitchen, some gremlins crawl out of the refrigerator and scare the snot out of me. On the stairs, a mouse wearing what looks like a prom gown is sliding down the banister. In my room, I see several fairies nesting in my bean bag chair. When I come in, they leap up and thumb their noses at me. I shriek and I think they shriek back—I can't hear them—and then they flit straight out through the walls.

Mostly, the next-door neighbors of alternate being go about their business and ignore me. I ignore them back as much as I can. But it's hard. It's hard to pay attention to things in my world with all the distractions. It's hard *not* to pay attention to the beings that aren't supposed to be in my world. But I have to learn to deal with it.

And I'm going to keep a sharp lookout for that caterpillar. If I ever see it, I'm going to wring its neck.

>
> summer getaway—
>
> building sand castles
>
> on Mars
>
> ~Lisa Timpf

Outside the Alien's Petting Zoo
Lauren McBride

tell me again

why I shouldn't pet

this sad-eyed ziago

oh (a hiss of pain)

the spines

Aliens, Magic, and Monsters
By Lauren McBride

Fun to read. Fun to write. *Aliens, Magic, and Monsters* features poems set in the unlimited and imaginative realm of science fiction, fantasy, and horror. The poems were chosen to showcase over twenty poetic forms from acrostiku to zip, from strict rhyme to free verse, and much more in between. There are guidelines included on how to write each type of poem. Try a sci(na)ku. At only six words, it's sure to interest even the youngest readers.

Type: Juvenile and Young Adult Poetry Manual
Ordering links:
Print: https://www.hiraethsffh.com/product-page/aliens-magic-and-monsters-by-lauren-mcbride

ePub: https://www.hiraethsffh.com/product-page/aliens-magic-and-monsters-by-lauren-mcbride-2

PDF: https://www.hiraethsffh.com/product-page/aliens-magic-and-monsters-by-lauren-mcbride-1

Trail of the Dancing Dinosaur
Pamela Love

Back on Earth, weather control means rain falls only late at night. Most people, including me, hardly ever saw it. My little brother, Ty, never did.

But now my family lives on Preska, one of Earth's colony worlds, where rain is common. Today we had something called a *downpour*. I'd never even imagined so much rain—it felt like someone was dumping an ocean on top of our home. Giant ferns, called megaferns, outside our window bowed down under the weight of all that water.

Our comm unit buzzed. My brother answered. "Mackenzie House."

"Hello, Ty. Is Ava in the room?" It was Mom. When I said hello, she went on, "Because the weather's so rough, I'm staying with my patient at the mainland settlement. It's not safe to risk an aircar flight until the storm's over, which should be tomorrow morning. Ava, you're in charge until I get back." She didn't bother telling us to stay indoors. Ty and I always find some excuse to keep out of any rain heavier than a sprinkle.

"Okay, Mom." She cut the comm and I sighed, wishing our family lived in the settlement with the other colonists. But our folks wanted the *privacy*—that's an old-fashioned word meaning being by ourselves —they had found on a small island nearby, just for our family.

"Ava, when's Dad coming home? I miss him." Ty stared out the window as if he could see our father, who was on a solo journey to explore a much larger island hundreds of kilometers away.

"Just three more days to wait." Ty slumped against the glass. Patting him on the shoulder, I said, "Imagine how many new plant species he must've found. Maybe we can write a report about them for school and get extra credit."

Ty pouted. "Plants are boring. Discovering dinosaurs would be more fun."

I shook my head. "Sorry. Before Preska was colonized, satellites scanned it for large animals—" The comm unit buzzed again. This time I answered. *Mom probably forgot to tell us something.* "Hello?" Static crackled. "Hello?" Still no answer.

"Who is it, Ava?"

"Probably Mom checking on us. Storms interfere with comm units. Anyway, Dad said that satellites didn't find anything larger than a goat." Outside, something gave a weird shriek.

"What's that?" Ty demanded.

"It's an Earth animal. It looks like—"

"I know what a goat is." He rolled his eyes. Ty's smart for eight. "I saw a picture when I was learning the alphabet. What was that noise? I've never heard the wind sound like that."

Neither had I, but I didn't know, either. There's still so much we don't know about our new world. "Maybe it's a dinosaur, after all—it could've been hiding under a *really* big fern."

Something slick and slimy brushed against my ankle. One look and I let out a groan. "Skitterers!" They're mobile, worm-like seeds of a Preskan plant. Three weeks after the colonists landed here, we'd assembled forty shelters for people and supplies. Then the skitterers sprouted. Their roots tore apart more than half of the buildings. None were undamaged.

Yanking open the door, I pulled the skitterers off my hands—not an easy job. Their tendrils are strong. I smashed them with a rock we keep there for just that reason. "I'll find where they blew in. Ty, see if more got inside."

Fifteen minutes later, I'd sealed a crack by a window. "Any more skitterers, Ty? Ty?"

No answer. *He couldn't have gone outside!* But a quick check of our closet showed he had taken his rain gear. Gritting my teeth and grabbing my own gear plus a flashlight, I dashed into the rain, following his tracks and shouting my brother's name over the wind's roar. "Ty! Where are you?"

Soon my shouts were echoing off the megaferns. At least the lightning had passed over. *Just wait until I find him...*

"Ty!" Of course, he probably couldn't hear me over the storm noise, but I had to let out my frustration. And as bad as the storm was, it still felt *good* to yell. Back on Earth, there are just too many people. Kids learn early on to keep their voices down, or nobody could stand the noise. "Come on, it's dangerous out here!" I wouldn't have minded being alone with Ty during the storm, as loud as it was, if only we'd been indoors. Instead, he went outside to chase a dinosaur. *And whose fault is that, Ava? Who decided to be funny?*

"Oh!" I'd stumbled into an ankle-deep hole. I'd never seen mud before I came to Preska (or many holes, either), and this was the first time I'd ever touched the stuff. It felt slimy and squishy, like a skitterer. Before I shouted something that *wasn't* Ty's name, guess who turned up?

"Ava! You were right!" Ty pointed. Whatever had made the "hole" had claws, four around its more or less round foot. My brother swung his flashlight's beam over the ground. "Look at all the dinosaur footprints. There's one over there and two more that way!" He giggled. "Maybe it was dancing."

I was stunned. It did look as if *something* huge and heavy had been jumping around. Those holes were *not* there yesterday. Several big ferns were knocked down, too. Maybe the wind had done it, but I'd never seen a fallen fern here. *It does look like a brontosaurus was doing ballet.* Reaching for Ty's hand, I said, "Let's go."

"Don't you want to follow that trail? What if a dinosaur's here?" he whined.

"And what if it's hungry? Move it!"

A megafern came crashing down, missing us by centimeters. My heart almost stopped, but at least Ty quit arguing. Scrambling over the plant, we half-ran, half-slid through the mud back to our home. Panting, I shut the door.

Buzz.

"Hello?"

"Ava, what's wrong?" Mom demanded.

"Nothing, Mom."

"Didn't you try to call me three times?"

"No, you called *me*...didn't you? I only heard static, though."

"That's all I heard, too. But it wasn't anybody in the settlement trying to reach me. I checked." She sighed. "Probably more storm interference. Lightning's coming closer here. See you tomorrow. Goodbye."

Ty starting jumping on the sofa. (No, he didn't take his muddy boots off first.) "Wait until she hears about the dinosaur! Wait until Dad does!"

I should've told him to clean up the mess he was making. Instead, I asked, "How could the satellites have missed something the size of a brontosaurus? Dad said those scanners are powerful enough to spot a mouse." For a moment I wondered if the alien monster could be invisible, but decided that was too hard to believe.

Bouncing onto the floor, Ty said, "Maybe lightning messed up the scans, like they do communicators."

I frowned, hating to admit that my little brother had figured out something faster than I could. But fair is fair. "Maybe you're right. When I told Mom about my call with only static on the other end, she said that she'd gotten three. She thinks this storm caused them somehow. All this wild weather is a lot of trouble—no wonder people invented a way to control it on Earth." Ty grinned. "Maybe the dinosaur was trying to call us." I sucked in my breath. "Ava?

What's wrong? Why are you looking at me like that?"

This time, Ty chased me outside. Together we ran to the "dinosaur's" tracks. I wanted a closer look at the broken megaferns.

Preskan ferns are flexible. Even in storms, they almost never break. "He must've gone that way," I muttered. Weaving through the forest, finally I held up my hand. "Shh." Listening hard, I heard a familiar humming. Moments later my flashlight's beam touched something large with clawed feet made to grip sometimes-slippery alien terrain: an aircar.

Ty shrieked louder than a dozen dinosaurs when he saw the number 555 on its side. "It's Dad!" We scrabbled onto the megafern lying against it. Both of us banged on the door. "Dad! Dad! Can you hear us? Are you okay?"

"Ava? Ty? I'm fine, but something's holding this door shut."

69

"It's a megafern. Ty, help me." It was a struggle, but we managed to bend it enough for Dad to squeeze out.

He chuckled as he hugged us. "I had a chance to come home early, but lightning surprised me before I could surprise you."

Shivering at the scorch marks running the length of his aircar, I said, "Oh, we're surprised, all right. Otherwise, I would've warned you about the storm."

"I called you and your mother, but I only heard static. Good thing you got my message anyway."

"But we didn't! Ava, how did you know Dad was the dancing dinosaur?" Ty demanded.

Dad raised his dripping eyebrows. "Dancing *dinosaur*?" Ty explained about the tracks. "Huh, I guess they would look like the trail of a brontosaurus. Actually, the lightning strike damaged my landing control system. That, plus the wind, bounced me around another clearing before I finally wound up here. What a ride! But how did you figure out I was home early?"

"With Ty's help." I smiled, not even brushing away the raindrops on my eyelashes. "That shriek we heard—he knew it wasn't wind. It must've been this aircar. He found its 'footprints', too. And when he said the dinosaur had called, I guessed it was you."

Ty stared. "But I was *joking!*"

Wicked Woods
Leigh Therriault

Under starless skies, they weaved
through wicked woods with
weary bones and empty bellies

until one by one, the children
disappeared.

Their names still rang hollow
many days later through
the misty thicket—

worried parents calling out
for their beloved to return.

until one by one, the children
reappeared...

in a different realm

    where nobody knew their names.

Stay Cool Danny
Hala Dika

"Approaching Kontara," the captain said, "Please remain seated until the spaceship has come to a complete halt."

I looked out the window, ravenous to catch a glimpse.

"Sit down Danny," my mother said, "You heard what the captain said."

"Well?" my father said, "This trip better be worth it, it cost enough."

"As you've said a thousand times dear," my mother replied.

"At any rate," he continued, "These aliens better put on a good show. God knows why else they exist?"

I stared at my father, not saying a word. He doesn't understand anything, I thought.

Alien cities were the most popular destinations in the galaxy. New-Human planets made deals with their boards of elders, telling them that under the cover of becoming tourist attractions, they would be considered less of a threat, and given special privileges. Having seen what humans could do, it did not take them long to decide. But having read one of their books, translated from the telepathic, I knew they were eons ahead of us. Still the humans on this ship had little to no use for mental evolution. All they wanted were some pictures, a Kontara mug, and a t-shirt.

When I finally caught a glimpse of the city from above, I stared bug-eyed. The tallest building was of a lava-like purple. And the surrounding land was lavender and green, with rivers cutting through. The others rushed to get their cameras. They pushed and jostled each other to get the best angle. Their flashing was so bright, I could hardly see. My father shoved me out of the way, leaning over me and taking a shot. "That's gonna be a good one," he said.

"It's beautiful isn't it?" I said.

He shrugged, "We might just get our money's worth."

"Now as soon as we get down there, we'll get some lunch," my mother said.

My father was already calculating the cost. "Do you suppose they have a MacDonald's?"

"Oh I'm sure they do," my mother replied, "All the comforts of home the ad said."

Soon their dragging conversation faded into the background. I wasn't looking for the comforts of home. I was looking for an adventure. I had brought my book with me and hoped I could find a Kontara boy who would answer all my burning questions. True this might be difficult with my parents along, but then again, I had fooled them before.

Walking into the Kontara space-port, I was shocked to find the Kontarians; a telepathically evolved race; carrying luggage, rolling buggies and wheel-chairs, and tending to and serving the needs of the tourists.

My father was very rude to them.

"Now you make sure those bags go to the right place boy," he said, "I did not come here to search for bags."

"Yes sir," the young alien said.

They have lowered themselves to speak our language, I thought. I smiled at the boy, ashamed. He stared into my eyes and grinned. "You're father's a real jerk," I suddenly heard in my head.

"I know," I thought without thinking. The young alien gave me a nod of respect. Had he heard me?

"Danny," my father said, "Wake up." As we walked away, he added, "These aliens aren't worth the green on their faces."

How he had decided this without talking to one of them first, I'll never know. I had just had a telepathic exchange, and he was still grumbling about luggage.

As we walked along, I stared into the eyes of other aliens, fascinated. My mother and father were arguing about something having to do with the hotel. I kept staring at the aliens. Suddenly, I heard a strange frequency. It was very calming; undulating, like slow waves. And then, just as suddenly, my parent's conversation was cut off, as if I'd gone deaf to it. All that remained was the frequency. And then I could do it, I could hear the aliens' thoughts!

"Humans," one of them said, "They treat us like cardboard cut-outs."

"Like we're only here for their amusement," replied another.

"They wouldn't know a mentally-evolved race from a hole in the ground," added a third.

Staring at my parents, I began to laugh.

"What's so funny?" my father asked me, breaking me out of this induced trance.

"Nothing," I said.

"Stay close," he replied, "I hear these Kontarians are always stealing human artifacts."

I was really starting to get annoyed with his little comments, and couldn't help myself. "Like what?" I asked, "Your antique water-bottle?"

"Don't start with me boy," he warned, "I'm in no mood."

The air-taxis were of a lava-yellow, swirling with black. They must have seen our old movies, and understood something of a retro-throwback. The alien piloting the machine with his mind, sat back, listening to my parents' conversation curiously. The alien laugh is quite giggly.

"Is it safe to touch the lava?" I thought.

"Go ahead kid," he replied, surprised I had picked up the telepathy so quickly.

I reached down and touched it. It seemed to react to my body organically; moving and swirling around my finger. "Wow." I said out loud.

"Wow what?" my father interrogated.

"The lava," I said, "It's amazing."

"What's the big deal," he said.

"Papa," I replied, "That alien is piloting this air-taxi with his mind."

"Humph," my father said, "Probably never did a day's worth of honest labor in his life."

"Your father is a real…" the alien thought.

"I know," I replied before he finished.

We flew over a special district. Looking down at it, my stomach began to turn. It looked exactly like every tourist area I'd ever seen. The same brand of hotels, restaurants, health spas, and tennis facilities.

"Well now," my father said, "This is more like it."

"They have a Panera," my mother replied, delighted.

I didn't bother to hide my disgust.

"Why are you rolling your eyes boy?" my father asked, "This isn't expensive enough for you?"

"Sure dad," I said, "It's great." He would never get it anyway, so why bother.

"If you want to see the real Kontara," the driver said only to me, "take the flashway to the Oriana District."

We reached the hotel and I watched the alien unload the bags. I rushed to help him, but my father pulled me away. "Let *it* do it," he said, "That's what *it's* here for."

"Dad!" I yelled.

"Not your fault," the alien replied, "Some folks are just born with their foot in their mouths."

I giggled, and my father gave me a stern look, as if to say, don't talk to them.

The district we were staying in reminded me of a cruise ship. They still had those. Instead of ocean, space; complete with massive buffets, giant chocolate fountains surrounded by heaps of fruit, swimming pools and water-slides, and a variety of second-class entertainment. Most people never left the tourist districts. But of those who did, there were three major sites they came to see; the Kontara Lava High-Tower, the Bezian Fruit Orchards (a fruit exclusive to Kontara), and the Plevia Oasis, a place whose beauty was said to be unparalleled.

My father, always complaining about getting his money's worth, would make certain we saw all three, and took enough pictures to prove it to the people back home. I did want to see all of these things, but not with my parents. They seemed to ruin everything. I was so sick of being told to see the world through their eyes. In their house, *I* knew something of being an alien.

The next morning, I sat on the edge of my bed, watching my parents get dressed and bicker. My father snapped his fingers in front of my face. "Come on, come on," he said, "Get moving, we want to hit the tower before the rush."

'Hit the tower', I thought, he doesn't get the point at all. Finally, I did what I always do, tuned them out and entered my own world, in thoughts they could neither see nor hear. I was about to see something truly magnificent, and I wasn't about to let them ruin it for me.

The flashway was packed with tourists. It moved so fast, you hardly felt as if you were moving at all. And when it stopped, you didn't feel the halt of the brakes. There was nothing to compare it to back home. Alien engineering was very smooth. Inside, the adults continued to bicker, but the children looked at each other with wide-eyed wonder. The little ones jumped in the aisle, singing, "Zoom, zoom, zoom," and laughing.

As it turned out, the high-tower was the same purple one I'd seen from the sky. It was strange to stand right next to it, for it seemed to be alive; an organism rather than a building. The floors were of a cooled lava, solid and shiny as glass. Inside was a museum, which included the natural history of the Kontara alien race. I was very excited to see it, and started to run inside, when my father stopped me.

"Wait!" he yelled, "Go stand next to your mother while I take this picture. The whole point of this thing is how high it is."

I really hated him then, and went to stand next to my mother, huffing and puffing all the way. What an Idiot! I kept saying to myself. My mother had that glazed, permanently smiling, look on her face. The one that made me wonder if she were really there at all. My father kept walking backward to get the whole tower in frame. To amuse myself, I imagined him walking towards the edge of a cliff, falling off, and screaming about not getting his money's worth all the way down. I laughed to myself at the thought. If it weren't for these little fantasies, I would've gone crazy.

Finally inside, I was left to my own devices, and told to meet my parents in the main area at such and such a time. I took the deep, relaxing breath, of freedom.

The place was similar to many of the natural history museums I had seen on school trips. It had scenes of Kontara evolution over time, displayed in life-like dioramas.

The first one, was of a people who looked human, but with very high foreheads. They were sitting around a glowing mineral, the way cavemen sat around a fire. I looked quickly at the plaque next to it. "The discovery of Lavite," it read, "The mineral which makes advanced evolution possible. The spark of all alien life."

I heard the very familiar sound of my bickering parents in the distance, and looked up to see that they were headed in my direction. I quickly hid behind something. I watched them arrive and stare at the scene. My father shrugged, and my mother still had that look on her face. Neither of them bothered to read the plaque. My father ordered my mother to stand in front of it, and snapped another picture. I shook my head and went on to the next scene.

In human history, it was not long after the discovery of fire, that it was used to forge weapons. But not so in Kontarian history. For the Lavite moved like lava, but was cool to the touch. And being a kind of living substance, seemed to have a peaceful will of its own.

"The Lavite itself," read one of the plaques, "is evolutionary."

My mind was ablaze with questions. I had never imagined such technology. Again I saw my parents coming and hid. Again my father snapped a few pictures and didn't bother to read the plaque. I decided to go get some lunch, hoping that afterwards, they would be further ahead of me, and I could take my time.

There were burgers and chips and B.L.Ts for the tourists. But I wanted to try Kontara cuisine. There was only one counter which served it. I sat down, and an alien in a white-apron approached. He spoke to me in English, with the air of a diner. "What'll it be?" he asked.

I stared at the menu. "I think I'll try the Kontara Special," I said.

"One Kontara Special!" he yelled to the other alien.

He brought me a tiny plate, with what looked like three beans on it.

"Bread, main course, dessert," he said, pointing to each one. Then he gave me a small fork. There was not much need for a napkin.

I took a bite of the first bean, sure enough it tasted like bread! Warm, buttery bread, fresh from the oven. It was so good, I closed my eyes with pleasure, savoring the flavor.

"Good huh?" the alien asked.

"Unbelievable," I replied.

The main course was like nothing I'd ever tasted before. It was hot and delicious, and seemed to fill all the senses at once, so that you felt a warm, fulfilled glow everywhere. And the dessert? Tasted like it had been made by the hands of an angel. But when I'd finished eating the beans, I was still hungry.

"Wait," the alien told me.

I did. All of a sudden, the flavors came back to me, in the order they were meant to be eaten. They came in three or four flavor waves, with the dessert last. I stared up at him in amazement.

He smiled, "Full?"

"Yeah," I replied, stunned.

I looked at the clock. I had one hour left to myself. As I was walking back to the natural history exhibit, I heard an alien speaking in very good English. I looked over and found he was surrounded by a group of tourists, giving them a tour of, and explaining Kontara Alien Art. Seeing he was around my age, fourteen or fifteen, I decided to join them.

"And this piece is entitled, "Wormhole", he explained, pointing to a very strange painting. Suddenly, he put half his arm inside it. It seemed to have no back. He pulled it out. "The artist here," he went on, "Amu Berdeen, wanted you to experience the strange pull of the wormhole." The tourists were mesmerized. One by one they tried it. I stayed with them until the end of the tour, and decided I wanted to talk to the boy.

"Hey?" I said, "That was a really good tour."

"Thanks," he replied, "I do my best."

"You can say that again," I thought, forgetting who I was with.

"I do my best," he repeated, grinning. He stared at me. "Your telepathy is very good," he said, "How old are you in human years anyway?"

"Almost fifteen," I replied.

"Then you are what they call a teen-*ager*?"

"Yes," I said.

"Do you mind if I practice my human teenage lingo with you?" he asked.

"Not at all," I said.

"That's what's up!" he replied, grabbing my hand in some kind of strange teenage-alien handshake. "What are you doin right now?" he asked.

"I'm supposed to meet back up with my parents," I replied, hating the idea.

"Oh?" he said, "What a drag."

I looked up at him surprised. "Parents are a drag here too?" I asked.

"Kid," he said, "Parents are a drag everywhere."

"Can I ask you something?" I asked.

"Shoot," he said.

"Does your father hate humans the way mine hates aliens?"

"I wouldn't say hate," he said, "I mean he gets weary of them from time to time. But he says there is no stopping alien-human interaction anymore. And that aliens have been aware of humans far longer than humans have been aware of aliens. He says we have to understand this and take them one at a time."

"Kinda like you're doin with me," I said.

"Pretty much."

There was a short silence. "Hey?" he said, "If you're into disobeying your parents for the day, I could take you down to the Oriana District?"

I recognized the name and smiled. "Yeah! I'm into that!" I replied.

"Cool," he said.

I waited outside the employee dressing room. He came out wearing a leather vest and some blue jeans, white sneakers on his feet. I thought he was the coolest person I'd ever seen, alien or otherwise.

"What's your name anyway?" I asked.

"Carcuula," he replied, "But they call me Cuul."

"Cool."

As we were walking out, I could see my parents at a distance, still bickering, my father looking at his watch and fuming. I put my hand over my mouth and laughed, following Cuul.

The flashway wasn't so busy this time. The Oriana District was four stops away, five seconds in flashway. Walking out, I had a familiar feeling of the downtowns back home. There were movie theaters, bars, clubs, and live music.

"So what do you want to do first?" Cuul asked.

"You pick," I replied.

"Music," he said, "Definitely music."

He took me to a place called, Ankala's. I could already hear the place was jumpin. The aliens in there were hoopin and hollerin to some kind of music which had the echo of Jazz. I only knew this because my uncle was an Old-Earth collector of things they used to call records, and he let me listen to some on a very old machine.

"They use their voices here?" I asked.

"It's one of the only place they do," he said, "After all, music requires sound, and an audience that let's you know how you're doin every once in a while."

We sat at a table and Cuul ordered two drinks, a bluish-yellow concoction.

"Whaddya call these?" I asked, holding up my glass.

"Sunny-Skies," he replied, "Gives you a smooth, warm high, and you never have to worry about hangovers. No alcohol."

I took a sip and it wasn't long before I was feelin good. A new act took the stage and I looked up to see This Sunny-Skies stuff is strong, I thought, rubbing my eyes in disbelief. But the image remained the same. I stared at Cuul, pointing to the stage. "Is that who I think it is?" I finally asked.

"John Coltrane?" he said, as if it were no big deal, "Yeah."

I stood up and stared wide-eyed. "He looks just like he did on my uncle's album cover," I said, "How did you bring him back?"

"He had an alien encounter before he died," Cuul said, "We took some DNA samples, and mixing it with some alien matter, he was reborn in one of our laboratories."

"I guess you must really like his music here," I said, still disoriented.

"Well he was always ahead of his time," Cuul said, " The Alien Council for the Arts felt that he wasn't finished evolving musically, and were curious to see how far he would take it with more time."

"Awesome," was all I could say.

"Turned out," he went on, "that he was as silent as the rest of us, only communicating through his horn."

I couldn't believe the sound, I had never heard anything like it. It was incredible. "What's that he's playing?" I asked.

"It's called Lavite Jazz," he replied, "As you can see, his saxophone is made from the substance. They are synchronized as one. The Lavite absorbs the vibrations of everything around it. It feeds him moods and emotions. And with these he improvises."

"But the sound?" I asked.

"It's half human, half alien," he said, "The tones are telepathic."

Sure enough, when I covered my ears, I heard them in my head, clear as a bell!

Afterwards, we met up with some of Cuul's friends. They seemed to have a thing for human clothes, music, and pop-culture from various ages. Cuul introduced me to some of them, and they too were very excited to try out their human-teenage lingo.

"Yo Danny?" one of them asked, surprising me, "What's good son?" It was an older lingo, but not difficult to translate.

There was a teenage-alien girl there named Safia. She seemed to take a liking to me and sat down next to me. "I've never met a human boy before," she said.

"Well we're pretty much all the same," I replied.

"Naaw," she said, "You're different, I can tell."

I blushed. She was wearing a tight pink shirt, rouge lipstick, and a white shell necklace. Her black eyes shone with life, and my heart started to beat really fast.

"You're cute," she said.

I was very nervous, but tried my best to keep the conversation going. "You got some sky here," I said, "I can even make out planets that I never could back home."

"There is nothing like the Kontara sky," she agreed, "It is even more ancient than your Old-Earth pyramids."

"How ancient?" I asked her.

"Since before human history," she replied, "We have been evolving for a much longer time than you."

"You must think I'm some kind of dummy huh?" I asked.

"Not at all," she replied, "Love is always evolved."

She said love, I thought, again forgetting who I was with.

But she did not shame me, and only smiled, her eyes still shining. We stared at each other for a while, and before I knew it, I was drawn into a kiss; my very first. Afterwards, we held hands and stared at the sky.

Cuul came over grinning from ear to ear. "I see you've met Safia," he said.

I blushed again.

"Did you still wanna get back before sun-up?" he asked.

"How can I contact you?" I asked her.

"Do you have a telescope?" she said.

"Yes!" I replied eagerly.

"Just point it towards Kontara and think of me. You will hear my thoughts, and I will hear yours."

I kissed her once more, for a little longer.

"Come on lover boy," Cuul said.

We walked toward the flashway. "Your friends are really cool," I said, "I wish I was that cool."

My new friend stopped. "You are that cool Danny," he said.

"Not back home," I replied, "I'm not one of the popular kids."

"You think being cool has anything to do with popularity?" he asked me. "It doesn't.

It's about accepting people for who they are no matter how different, and having the courage to get to know them and judge for yourself. And as far as I'm concerned, that makes you the coolest person I know."

"Thanks man," I said, uplifted.

We climbed the stairs and boarded the flashway.

"You had a good time?" Cuul asked, as we sped along.

"Best time of my life," I replied.

Back in the tourist district, we stood on the platform, awkward, the way all teenage boys were when it came to goodbyes.

"I'll remember you," Cuul finally said.

"Me too," I replied.

He nodded his head and hopped back on the flashway. Hanging outside the open door, he waved.

"Stay cool Danny," he said.

Who?

Michelle St. James is a published author and artist, whose artwork has appeared on the covers of Factor Four, Pulp Literature, ParSec Magazine, Tree and Stone, The Maul Magazine, Radon, and Spaceports & Spidersilk. Her YA novel, *The Mermaid of Agawam Bay*, is available on Amazon. Check out more of her art on www.stjames-art.com

Dave Aronlee lives in California with his family. He loves dragons and volleyball and is a lawyer, but would dearly love to be a fantasy writer when he grows up.

Cheryl J. Brown has been a lover of literature since childhood. She studied mass communication and psychology at Winthrop University. Over the years she has written a plethora of short stories and poetry. Her specialty genres are horror and sci-fi. She lives in her head, no location is needed, you can always find her working and reading with her beloved dog, Pepper, by her side.

Laurel Hanson is an aspiring writer from Maine who lives by the advice offered by Lewis Carroll that one should "believe in as many as six impossible things before breakfast.'

Pamela Love was born in New Jersey, and worked as a teacher and in marketing before becoming a writer. Her work has appeared in various children's publications, including Spaceports & Spidersilk, Cricket, and Highlights for Children, among others. She is a member of the SCBWI, and won that organization's 2020 Magazine Merit Fiction Award for "The Fog Test", which appeared in Cricket. She lives in Maryland.

Drew Alexander Ross resides in Los Angeles, where he works as a script analyst. Drew has over ten placements in screenwriting contests and over ten short story publications, including short stories featured in The British Fantasy Society's Horizons Magazine, Mythic Magazine, Door = Jar Magazine, and Bewildering Stories.

Hala Dika is a poet and author who lives for a good adventure. Her work has been published or is upcoming for Yellow Mama, Schlock!, Mobius Blvd, Aphelion, TallTaleTV, Black Cat Weekly, the Lovecraftiana

Halloween Anthology, and Dragon Soul Press's Fairy Rites Anthology. You can connect with her via her Amazon Author's page and Twitter below.
https://www.amazon.com/author/haladika
https://x.com/adventurebard

Gary Davis enjoys exercising his imagination through crafting dark and darkly humorous poetry and short stories. In a given poem, he likes to combine narrative, emotion and image in a rhythmic tapestry with hopefully a twist at the end. Mr. Davis has published poetry in *Spaceports & Spidersilk, Tales from the Moonlit Path, Scifaikuest, Star*Line, Tales of the Talisman, Bloodbond, Illumen, It Came from Her Purse, Potter's Field, The Hungur Chronicles*, and a sci-fi anthology, *Kepler's Cowboys* (2014-2024). He has published ten short stories also (2016-2024).

Adele Gardner (they/them, Mx., gardnercastle.com) has poetry and fiction in Analog Science Fiction and Fact, Clarkesworld, Strange Horizons, PodCastle, and Flash Fiction Online, among others, and a poetry collection, Halloween Hearts, published by Jackanapes Press. Twelve poems won or placed in the Poetry Society of Virginia Awards, Rhysling Award, and Balticon Poetry Contest.

Lisa Timpf's speculative poetry has appeared in a variety of magazines and anthologies, including New Myths, Star*Line, Eye to the Telescope, Liquid Imagination, and Polar Borealis. When not writing, Lisa enjoys organic gardening, bird-watching, and walking her lively Jack Russel-cocker spaniel Chet. You can find out more about Lisa's writing at http://lisatimpf.blogspot.com/.

Margaret Zotkiewicz is a graduate of the University of Dayton and the Institute of Children's Literature. Her articles and short stories for children have been published in "Skipping Stones.org", "Guardian-Angel-Kids", "Spaceports and Spidersilk", "Cadet Quest", "White Cat", and "Primary Treasure". She is a member of Julie Foster Hedlund's 12 x 12 Picture Book Challenge, and the Society of Children's Book Writers and Illustrators, Northern Ohio chapter. Her poem "My Animal Ball" won Fifth Place in the 2024 Institute of Children's Literature Rhyming Animal Poetry Contest. In her non-writing free time, Margaret enjoys reading, creating things with her hands, following the burgeoning Toledo music scene, and traveling with her family.

Lauren McBride is author of the chapbook *Aliens, Magic, and Monsters* (Hiraeth, 2023). Nominated for the Best of the Net, Pushcart, Rhysling, and Dwarf Stars Awards, her poetry has appeared internationally in speculative and mainstream publications including *Asimov's*, *Fantasy & Science*

Fiction, and *Utopia Science Fiction's 5th Anniversary Anthology.* She enjoys swimming, gardening, baking, reading, writing, and knitting scarves for U.S. troops.

Leigh Therriault is a writer and poet based in Ottawa, Canada. She is a graduate of the University of Toronto's Creative Writing Program and UC San Diego's Children's Book Writing Program. She is a member of SCBWI and the Canadian Authors Association, where she volunteers as the social media coordinator for the National Capital Region. Her writing for young readers appears in *The Caterpillar, The Dirigible Balloon, The Toy, Paddler Press,* and *Cricket.* Leigh lives with her family near an enchanted duck pond and enjoys watching the geese land at dusk.

www.ingramcontent.com/pod-product-compliance
Lightning Source LLC
LaVergne TN
LVHW010407070526
838199LV00065B/5912